my little Pony

Pinkie Pie's Special Day

By Jennifer Christie

Illustrated by Lyn Fletcher

HarperFestival®

A Division of HarperGollins Publishers

Ponyville was buzzing with excitement.
The ponies were planning a big surprise party
for their friend Pinkie Pie!

The morning of the surprise, the ponies woke up very early.

They could hardly wait for the party to start.

Outside, the sky was blue and the air smelled sweet, like cotton candy.

"Today is the day!" said Rainbow Dash.

"Pinkie Pie will be so surprised!" the other ponies added.

Rainbow Dash held up a glittery tutu and whirled around the room.

Toola-Roola patted her hair and put on sparkly purple socks.

They had to look their best for the big day!

The ponies wanted to show Pinkie Pie how much they loved her,
because she was their best friend. She always made everyone smile.
Today Pinkie Pie's friends wanted to make her happy, too!
"Let's wake up Pinkie Pie," said Rainbow Dash.

Pinkie Pie's room was pink, pink, pink.
When the ponies came in, their special friend was still fast asleep.
"Good morning, Pinkie Pie!"
said Rainbow Dash.

"Oh my! Why are you all here so early?"
asked Pinkie Pie, as she rubbed her eyes.
"The sun is up," said Rainbow Dash. "We should go outside and play."
The other ponies cheered.

"Hurry up and get ready, Pinkie Pie,"
said Toola-Roola. "We have lots to do!"
The ponies were excited to be with Pinkie Pie.

They danced around the room happily.

Pinkie Pie twirled and put on her favorite summer dress.

Then all the ponies followed her outside.

"I've got an idea. Let's decorate Ponyville!" said Pinkie Pie.

"Yes!" agreed the ponies.

They all had lots of fun playing and decorating.

Pinkie Pie created a beautiful banner.

After a while, Pinkie Pie noticed that
she and Toola-Roola were the only ones around.
Toola-Roola's job was to keep Pinkie Pie busy while the others
prepared the surprise party. Toola-Roola started to put up the
banner that Pinkie Pie had made, when suddenly it slipped!

"Oh no!" cried Toola-Roola.

"What's the matter?" Pinkie Pie asked.

"I was putting up this banner,
and it just . . . it fell!" said Toola-Roola.

Pinkie Pie smiled. "Don't worry," she said,

"we can fix it together."

Pinkie Pie forgot about the other ponies
while she helped Toola-Roola put up the banner.
When they were finished, though, she began to worry.
"Where is everyone?" she asked.
"Um, I'm not sure," said Toola-Roola, nervously.
She did not want to ruin the surprise.

"Let's find the others," said Pinkie Pie.

She always wanted to make sure everyone was okay.

This was part of what made Pinkie Pie such a good friend.

The two ponies went in search of their friends.

Toola-Roola was finding it very hard to hide her excitement.
Pinkie Pie will be so surprised! she thought.

Toola-Roola and Pinkie Pie walked
past tiny butterflies and fragrant flowers.
Ponyville is especially beautiful today, thought Pinkie Pie,
but where is everyone?

Nearby, the other ponies finished preparing for the party.

"Oh! I hear them coming," whispered Rainbow Dash.

"Everyone, go hide," said Scootaloo.

Pinkie Pie and Toola-Roola reached a lovely area
filled with trees and flowers.
Suddenly Rainbow Dash and all of Pinkie Pie's friends
jumped out from their hiding places.
"Surprise, Pinkie Pie!" the ponies yelled all at once.

"It's a special party just for you!" said Toola-Roola.
Pinkie Pie looked confused. "I didn't expect a party!" she said.
She looked around and saw a beautiful pink cake.
There were bunches of bright pink balloons,
streamers, and other decorations!

"We want to thank you for being such
a wonderful friend," said Rainbow Dash.
Pinkie Pie was quiet for a moment. "Goodness! This is why you all
disappeared. And, Toola-Roola, you knew all along!"

"All the decorations are beautiful and pink just like you,
Pinkie Pie," said Toola-Roola.

Toola-Roola brought over Pinkie Pie's lovely banner!
It matched perfectly with the theme of the day.
Now the ponies just needed a game to play.
"Let's play musical chairs!" said Pinkie Pie.

The ponies pranced around to a happy song.
When the music stopped, they all found chairs to sit in,
except for Toola-Roola!
"Oh, Toola-Roola! Maybe next time," Starsong said.

"Thank you, everyone! You've made me so happy,"
Pinkie Pie said to her friends.
"You make us happy every day, Pinkie Pie!"
the ponies answered together.
All the ponies hugged, happy to be sharing
in Pinkie Pie's special day.